THE GLOWING LIGHT

"This is a story of a man's trials through life. The tribulations, mistakes that we all delve into and the presence of a man's strength and his weaknesses. This story may be outlandish in premises, but relevant to us all."

TRAVIS WATERS

AuthorHouse™
1663 Liberty Drive
Bloomington, IN 47403
www.authorhouse.com
Phone: 1 (800) 839-8640

Published by AuthorHouse 07/10/2019

ISBN: 978-1-7283-1843-1 (sc)
ISBN: 978-1-7283-1844-8 (e)

Print information available on the last page.

This book is printed on acid-free paper.

authorHOUSE®

A bright, white light glows in the air and a voice is heard.
A man emerges and begins to speak...

PART 1:

I've seen this light many times in my life. My name is Payton Brannon James. I was named "Payton" because my father always liked the Chicago Bears' running back wearing the number 34 jersey named Walter Payton, but everybody who knows me calls me PB & J. This is my story. I was born in the early 80's, but my life only lasted for a few decades. Some may say that I still exist, but the life that I have and once had doesn't seem the same anymore. We'll get back to that; let's just start at the beginning.

I was born like any other baby; in a hospital to a mother surrounded by doctors. [I'd guess; I don't really remember that day too much!] My father named Ricky Lynn James was a "man's man." One of those hard-asses who never showed any emotion about anything. He was a big, burly man with a rugged, black beard. Ricky and I didn't have too much in common. Even though we looked alike, we were complete opposites. He was a mechanic and an outdoorsman. He could take a transmission apart and put it back together or set up a campsite in five minutes. To his disappointment, I knew nothing about cars or how to set up a tent. I guess that may be why we weren't close either.

Unfortunately, he was a drunk also. The slim memories that I have of him always had him carrying a beer. The few times I got to ride in a car with him, he always had a beer between his legs. I even remember the times he would open a beer and let me sip the foam off the top of it. That probably didn't affect me too much because I think every child remembers their dad letting them do that. When Ricky let me sip the foam off his beer, it was my chance to feel close to him. One of the few that I ever felt.

I always liked sports and everything to do with sports. From collecting baseball cards, watching games on TV, to making a target out of duct tape on the brick wall of our house and throwing a tennis ball at it for hours. Hell, if I wasn't trying to sink a free throw shot at our basketball goal or loading up a baseball on a tee and seeing how far I could hit it, I even remember simply throwing a ball up in the air and catching it with my glove. I loved sports.

As I grew up, I played on many teams. Hell, I could play any sport and I was good. I was what they considered an "athlete." I remember the dominant feeling of the first homerun that I had ever hit to the humiliation of the first time that a baseball broke my nose. I even liked all the school stuff. I made straight A's and never got into any trouble. I was that kid in class who got to fold the school flag in the mornings and chosen to lead the kids to the cafeteria to eat lunch. Many of the students probably hated my guts for it, but I was always content.

I was the kid that one would say is a parents "wet dream." My mother could see that, but my father couldn't. I don't think he cared. I have a few good memories of my biological father and a few bad ones. It really doesn't matter. We all can say this. I was young...who cares?

My mother was a saint. Her name was Elaine Brannon, Elaine James after she married my father. She had me in her late twenties. I was her baby and she was my angel. Elaine was always there. She nursed all my wounds, attended all my sports games and all of my school functons. I was lucky to be born to her. My mother, who I called "Ma", dealt with all of the demands of having a child and a drunken husband. Just as an example, she would cook everyone dinner at 6 P.M., but my father wouldn't show up until 10 P.M. After she put me to bed, I could hear Ricky stumbling inside and the fighting would begin.

This seemed to happen every night, then I turned eight and my father my mother got a divorce. It appeared to be a new start, so I didn't take it too hard. Ma eventually started a long-distance relationship with a new man, so Elaine decided to marry and move to this new man's home. She and I moved down south...4 states from my father. Ricky didn't care. If it didn't have the incentive of alcohol along with a an easy woman, he didn't mind. Even though my ma was remarried to a new man and we lived in a new state, Ricky could've still seen me, but he never tried.

This man that ma had married was something special. Not in a "good way" either. He was always nice to me, played games and taught me a few things, but he wasn't so nice to my mother. He liked to hit women. He was devoutly religious and thought ALL women were beneath men. He was a dick...especially towards women.

I continued excelling throughout sports, the social life and school. Life wasn't so great at home. I remember him yelling and screaming at my ma. I didn't like him too much. In fact, I avoided any opportunity to be near the "dick." Through all of this, my ma survived and kept me safe. Elaine Thomas, her new married name, finally got a divorce from him when I was 15. It was well deserved and expected. No big deal to me. All I cared about is that she finally got away from what I assume was misery and transcended to her happiness. I don't know what ever happened to him. Who cares? Now let's get back to the story.

PART 2:

I led a normal life as a teenager. I went through that "rebellion stage" that all teenagers go through. I got in a little trouble. Letters sent home, trips to the principal's office and detentions. Nothing too bad that would affect anyone. I got an old 1987 Camaro that I fixed up to look like a hotrod. [Even though it only had a V6 engine. Don't tell anyone!] I chased a few girls like any boy would do, went to some parties with my friends where I would get drunk and smoke a variety of things. [Alluding to cigarettes and what they called "weed."] I had the life of cars, summer jobs, girls, and then my athletic life.

I was always a "large/athletically" built kid. It didn't hurt that I hit puberty at eleven. Hell, I was a 5'10" seventh grader with a half of a beard! So, I tried basketball. I was an average player. I was that boy you stuck under the goal to push other players around and get rebounds. Considering that I had already hit my growth spurt, I stopped growing and the other kids were catching up to me in height. The last game I remember playing, I heard my coach yelling: "Jump, James. Jump!" I didn't want to tell the coach that was the highest I could jump, but he figured it out soon. After that game, I never really played basketball again. Basketball was just for fun. I didn't really care that I never played again.

As for my true love that was the sport of baseball, I always loved to play it. I became a catcher and loved the player Carlton Fisk. I would watch every White Sox game that I could and mold my game after his. I was a hell of a catcher. No ball ever got by me and no runner could ever steal a base against me. Baseballs pelted my body, aluminum bats were slapped across my back. As for catchers, they called me a stud. I could hit the ball a mile, too. The "clean-up" hitter in your line-up was always me. I was even on a team that made it to the Little League World Series. We didn't win...damn Japan!

I did my best not to tell anyone, but by thirteen, I could feel my knees starting to hurt. I guess I had worn the cartilage down in my joints. I still played a few more years, but I wasn't the same. Therefore, I started to play a game called golf. I was good at it, but not great. The ball would travel a mile off my club, but the old saying is: "You drive for show, putt for dough." That saying was true for me. I could drive a golfball off the tee for 300 yards, but I couldn't make a 3 foot putt. My best score was +1. 73 isn't good enough to be anything special. I played a few years of that, made a few high school teams, but never took it seriously.

Normal so far, huh? Well, that's about to change.

PART 3:

One night when I was 16, my friends and I loaded up in my Camaro and decided to go play this new game called 'Laser Tag.' For those of you that don't know, it was just a game where every person put a vest on, ran around a maze, held these laser guns and shot at each other. The vest would count how many people you shot and how many times YOU were shot. It was awesome. It was like war. We all suited up and started shooting at each other...that's when my life changed.

As we were playing, it was dark and we all were creeping around to shoot each other. In the middle of this awesome, new game, I dropped and had some sort of seizure. I passed out. An ambulance came and got me and took me to a local hospital. I woke up in an emergency room with a light shining in my eyes.

That was the first time I saw the glowing light.

PART 4:

I had many tests done. MRI'S, X-rays, CT scans, EKG's, blood tests, etcetera. As many tests that they could run. Ma was sitting beside me in the hospital room when the doctors, all wearing white lab coats, entered. The doctors told me that I must have had a "bad reaction" to the lasers. I felt fine, they said I was fine, so I was sent home to live my life. All was well. My friends teased me, calling me "Laser Man" and "Seizure Boy", but I went back to my normal life.

That's when I met a girl in school. By all the "high school ways", we started dating. We always were together. I can't say much more about her except that she was my "high school sweetheart." Our relationship probably would have never lasted anyways, but I ended up cutting her off...eventually. We lasted a year, but she would end up being happier without me.

A few months later, I had an even worse "seizure" when I was asleep. Ma called the ambulance. I woke up in the ICU with a light glowing in my eyes.

That was the second time I ever saw the glowing light.

PART 5:

I didn't know what had happened. I was in a deep slumber and now I was in an hospital room. I went through all of the medical tests AGAIN. When I finished those tests, the doctors, still wearing those white lab coats, didn't know what was wrong with me either. All they had me do was schedule a test called an EEG. The sensors involved in an EEG were pasted on my scalp. I sat there for an hour as they must have been reading my brain waves. After days of waiting, the neurologist told me and my ma that I have what they call 'epilepsy.' A simple seizure disorder. This seemed more serious, but all I could do is believe what they told me. The doctors gave me a pill that I was to take daily and that would stop the "seizures." Okay. I took the pills and returned to my life. The pills were working. Even though my sophomore year of high school was almost over, I went back to school. Everything seemed fine. I still had my friends, my girlfriend and my ma. My life seemed normal again, but I always had this weird tingling on my right side. My ma scheduled a basic appointment with a neurologist. We asked the doctor what the weird tingling was. The doctor in a white lab coat said it was my body adjusting to the medication. Boy, was he wrong.

Other than the feeling I had on my right side, I felt okay. I was a 16 year-old living the teenage life. My grades never slacked too much, I still played on a few sports teams, I partied with my friends and stayed true to my "high school sweetheart." I thought all may be well. The medical community may have been correct. I guess I was wrong, but something didn't feel right. I hoped they were right, I was wrong and everything would return to normal. Yet I always had this feeling that something bad was coming.

PART 6:

About 6 months later, I turned 17 and everything seemed perfect. I had a slick-looking car, a nice summer job, a best friend, a serious girlfriend, graduation coming up and colleges to attend. My ma was there also. This may sound odd, but I wanted to be a psychologist. I was on my way.

Then that night came. I was asleep and had another 'seizure.' Ma called the ambulance. The 'seizure' was even worse. Again, I woke up in the ICU with a light glowing in my eyes.

That was the third time I ever saw the glowing light.

I was getting sick of this crap. Obviously, the pills they gave me didn't work. This 'seizure' was different though. I barely could feel the right side of my body. This was weird. I went through all of the doctor's tests again. I spent a few days in the hospital, then the doctors, still wearing white lab coats, walked in my room. They showed my ma and me a picture of my last MRI. I was told that I had an inoperable brain tumor. I had 6 months to live.

PART 7:

I couldn't believe it. I was always the best at everything I did. Now, this top-notch human would be dead. I, Payton Brannon James, "PB&J, would be alive no more. Like many others before me, I thought I would live until I was 80. I guess 17 years was it for me.

What was I going to do? I was never one for emotion, but, I have to admit, this rattled me. I lost everything in less than a year. I had two choices: I could give up and die aimlessly or I could finish the rest of my life with a little respect. Looking back, I guess I chose both.

Since I could barely walk without help, I gave up everything and everyone in my life. I quit my job, stopped driving, abandoned my friends and dumped my girlfriend. [This was the ending of the "high school sweetheart." I thought it would be best for her.] I became a "house-rat." I never talked to anyone, never went out of my house, but, for some reason, I completed high school. Luckily, the school system had a traveling teacher program. I was sent a nice man, about 50, with a bald head, glasses and a greying beard. He would drive to my house and home-schooled me. Other than my ma, he was the only person I ever talked to. After a few months, I completed high school and was declared a graduate. I finished school, but who cared? My ma, that was it. I never went to a prom or a graduation. My friends didn't care. In fact, after I left school, they all thought that I had died. I guess I brought that on myself. It was best for everyone to let me be and live their own lives, but I still felt invisible.

Part 8:

The time came. Six months had passed. Any day now, I was doomed to die. At that point, I didn't really care anymore. Whatever is beyond death, I was about to experience it. Tick-tock...I was waiting.

Six months turned into seven months. Seven months turned into eight months. Eight months into a year. One year into two years. I never died. Times were tough. I could barely walk, barely feed myself, barely bathe, barely dress myself. If it wasn't for my ma's help, I would've never made it. Yet, somehow I did. It was hard. It was harder than anything that I ever did. But I kept pushing. I kept having those night 'seizures', but I would never have them during the day. My right side got worse and worse and worse. Doctors were baffled. All of the "white coats" wanted to study me. Needless to say, they were stunned.

My ma, Elaine Brannon Thomas [my former stepdad's last name], came to me with a deal. She asked if I was willing to move to her parent's hometown in Missouri. She said that we would stop by one of the hospitals on the way so doctors could look at my brain. I didn't care. A move sounded good. The hospital was just a factor. So, we went. There we were. A moving truck packed with our things and driving off to Missouri. We drove for hours, but we made it. I was 19 and lived in the midwest.

The town we moved to was small. Our house was small as well, but she was finally happy. Her parents, her brother and her sister all within a couple of streets of each other. What did I care? Except for holidays and a few spontaneous visits to my family's homes, I never left the house. She was happy to feel safe at home. She deserved it.

A couple of days before, we stopped by a hospital in Arkansas. I took ALL of their tests again. A few weeks later, the white coats asked me to go to a local neurologist and see my results. They said that I didn't have a brain tumor anymore. In fact, the white coats said my whole body was fine. I was told to stop taking all of the meds that had been prescribed in my past. The doctors assumed all of my problems must be psychological. That began a new step in the story of my life.

PART 9:

Funny how I wanted to be a psychologist and now my problems merited a psychologist, huh? Well, an appointment was set up. I went. I went to about 30 different appointments in their offices. They tried to get me to cry, hypnosis, pills and many other things. Basically, they all said the same thing. I was diagnosed with a severe case of social anxiety, a psychosomatic disorder or a possible severe conversion disorder. Also, the psychologists said I had an "idolization for suicide." What that meant is that I was doing all of this to myself and I was hoping to end it with suicide. What crap! Why would I do this to myself? I just ignored them and kept that possibility in my head...even though we all knew it was crap.

I turned 21. Nothing had changed. I was still having night 'seizures.' My right side still didn't work correctly. I always was a skinnier, more muscular boy, but my body turned to goo. Given that all I could do was sit in a recliner, eat, read books and watch TV. What could anyone expect? I went from a taut 150 pounds to a 250 pound blob of fat. I was ashamed, but I didn't care. Without the use of my arm, what good was I? I was more trouble than an enjoyment.

PART 10:

Six months later, that all changed. I could walk again! My right arm started working! I could move! Four years that I had to deal with this ailment, but all of a sudden, without no explainable reason, it seemed to be over. I was so happy. If my muscles hadn't atrophied so much in the last four years, I would've skipped and danced around. It was probably the happiest feeling that I had ever felt. That was until I looked in the mirror. I was an obese, worned-down 21 year-old "man". I needed to fix this. I decided right then that I was going to lose weight and rebuild the muscles that I had lost.

I changed my diet. I had two pieces of fruit with a protein shake in the morning, a protein bar for lunch and boiled chicken with some sort of a vegetable along with a protein shake for dinner. Everyday, I exercised and lifted weights. I would spend hours locked in a room, working out. It was tough, but since my body was all of a sudden able to do this, I gladly did it. I did that for seven months in a row. Disregarding a few stretch marks and a battered figure, my once obese body had turned back into my teenage body...maybe even better. In seven months, I had lost 110 pounds! I had muscles again! Hell, I even had a six-pack stomach! It was time to move on, go out, meet some girls, have fun and maybe settle down some day. I did just that.

My first night out, I was alone and I went to a bar called "The Lounge." I noticed all the people in crowds of their friends, but I was the new guy in town. I ended up making friends quick thanks to Jesse.

The first night that I was out, an older man with grey hair and grey beard sat at the bar beside me. His name was Jesse Tyler. Honestly, he looked like a biker that was about to beat me up and steal my car. But, he was the nicest man that I had ever met. He simply asked me my name and if I wanted a smoke. I wasn't much of a smoker, but I went ahead and grabbed one from his pack. As we both gulped down a few beers, Jesse and I talked about everything ranging from the cliques in this town to where we lived at the moment. He had a couple more stories than I considering he was about 30 years older, but we bonded over his simple jester of asking me my name. Jesse had experience. He knew of whom to get involved, who to avoid and what every person's in that town intentions were. He was great guy and a very capable asset. Jesse was the epitome of what I eventually called a "good guy." From that moment on, we were always together. It was Jesse and Payton. He was my best friend and I was his best friend. He looked out for me; I tried to look out for him.

"The Lounge" was a good place for me. A quiet bar on the outside of town that was always busy, but not too busy. Due to Jesse's direction and advice, I even met a few ladies throughout that small town, but that's also where I discovered how much I had a hankering for alcohol. I loved it. It made me the man that I always wanted to be...I think. I drank booze like a sponge soaking up water. It led me to be free. I had a few wild nights under its spell, but we've all had those. Those stories, at least the ones I can remember, are for a different time.

About five months later, that man that I loved like a brother had a heart attack. Jesse passed away at the age of 54. I was heartbroken, but hearing all of the stories that he had told me about his younger days, his present days and the family he once had, I could understand. Neither of us were very religious men, but considering the true sadness that he had expressed, I would be mistaken in not thinking that the great man I called Jesse didn't deserve some eternal peace. I truly hope he found it...

PART 11:

A few months later, I decided to go to a state university. It was about 45 minutes away, but I found a nice apartment. The new home wasn't anything special. A two bedroom about 10 minutes away from my new school, but I was finally on my own. I still did all of my exercises. That's what I used that extra room for. I got an older, small car. It was blue, but it was durable; enough for me to get along. I was breezing through school. No problems yet. In the time that I was gone, my ma even met a new guy.

I'll never forget the first time I saw him. I was visiting my ma. I was driving through that small town and saw a man walking down the road. He was wearing these little pants, a tight shirt and white socks pulled up to his knees. I made some kind of joke to my ma about some guy that I just saw and what would make a person wear that outfit. She didn't laugh. She just looked worried. As I sat on her couch, we gossiped and I heard all the town news. Right then, I heard a knock at the door. My grandparents came into the house with this man in little shorts, a tight shirt and knee-high socks. I didn't know anything of him, but he was my ma's new boyfriend. His name was Monte Calvin. Monte eventually became my ma's third marriage. Thanks to Jesse, he was what I considered a "good guy". Just what my ma needed at the time.

I still had a couple of night 'seizures', but it wasn't anything that I couldn't handle. Life was back to normal. In this new college town, I made a few friends, had a few parties, met a few ladies; all was good. But as time went by, I could feel that weird sensation in my right side again.

I figured [and hoped] that unforgettable sensation would pass. I felt like my old self again, so it must just be a weird feeling, right? I was wrong. The only thing that seemed to calm my nerves and ease my pain anymore was alcohol.

On my 24th birthday, my ma and her new husband visited. [Don't worry. He was wearing different clothes!] By that time, I pretty much accepted him. After my ma and Monte left, I still had my whole night ahead of me. I went to this local dance bar that I had attended a few times. After a few drinks, that's when I saw her.

Her name was Sherri Johnson. She had an aura around her that pulled at my heart like no other woman had ever had. Sherri was a great-looking woman. A perfectly tanned face lined in wavy brown hair, a perfectly shaped body that fit well into her dark blue jeans and off-white shirt. Plus, she had a pair of crystal blue eyes that could that could melt iron. She was a little older than I, so I was afraid to speak to her. A friend of mine came up to me and told me that she was single, so I stumbled errantly over to where she was standing and spoke to her. What was I going to say? I didn't have some magical pick-up line, but I had to try for every man's bluborous methods. I had noticed previously that we were watching each other the whole night. All I could think to say her was:

"So, why did you stop looking at me?"

Pretty lame, huh? Well, it was a starter's line, but I think it may have worked. Maybe she felt sorry for me, but she talked to me for the rest of the night. She was a classy girl, so instead of trying to take her home at the end of the night, I just asked for her phone number.

The next day, I sat down in my little apartment, prepared myself and called the number that she had given me. She actually answered! We nervously chatted back and forth for about an hour. I told her SOME of my life history, she told me her's. I felt like I may be too needy or encroaching on her time, but I finally asked her out on a date. She was hesitant at first. I couldn't blame her after what she told me.

Sherri's story was fierce to me. In fact, it actually cut me like a newly sharpened blade, but it wasn't enough to make me run. She honestly told me that the last man that she was involved with used to do drugs, beat her and would cheat on her with any girl that was willing and near. I mean ANY GIRL. I thought that information was all that was going to be relayed in my direction, but she continued. Sherri told me even more of her story. It ended as such: she received a knock on her door one evening. It was the "crazy" girl of the neighborhood. She told Sherri that she was pregnant with Sherri's boyfriend's child! It sounded like a Jerry Springer show. I couldn't believe it at first, but after hearing the details of that man, I wasn't surprised. He was what Jesse would list and consider as a "bad man".

Little did I know, sweet Sherri was the last lady I would ever ask out again. A few months later, she walked into my little apartment that was decorated as a "man's apartment." I had a TV, a couch and a recliner surrounded by sports memorabilia. Sherri sat down on my worn out, tan with woven black checkers couch. I could tell she was nervous. I thought for sure she was going to break up with me. Instead, she told me she was pregnant. I had never felt a happiness like that. I had finally made a family of my own...

PART 12:

I called her father to ask permission to marry her. I thought it was the correct way of handling the entire situation, but he seemed confused by my methods of proposal. His answer was: "I guess so." Good enough! I asked for her hand on Christmas. I wrote out some lovey-dovey words on a card with a black jewelry box placed in the center. Inside of it was single diamond engagement ring. Sherri and I got engaged. She moved into my little apartment. [She redecorated it.] Seven or eight months later, we were married and she had a little boy. There wasn't any doubt about it, the boy was mine. Even though the baby had her blue eyes, he looked just like me. On our way from the hospital with a newly born infant, I silently claimed that this was my life now. A wife, a baby and a place to live.

Unlike my father, I was there. I did all of the "fatherly" things. Even though I couldn't change a diaper because I gagged everytime I saw or smelled poop. [And yes, she laughed at me everytime I gagged over poop.] I still did all I could do. Three months after that, Sherri was pregnant again with a little girl. We moved into a new place [decorated for babies by her]. A three bedroom apartment across town. A humble little place, nothing special. Seven months later, there we stood. A husband and a father, a wife and a mother, a 1 year-old and a newborn. In less than two years, I went from a ramblin' bar-hopper to a new dad of two children.

PART 13:

I was now 26 and on the verge of being an old man. Something like that would never be a matter to me because I was happy. I thought I was settled. Little did I know, a new marriage with two kids wasn't easy. Sherri and I had our little spats; nothing major. But about a year later, Sherri and I got into a big fight. I don't even remember what it was about; probably something stupid. We argued like never before. It probably didn't help that we were drunk at the time, but we kept fighting for hours. I've lived by one rule in my life: NEVER HIT A WOMAN. Unfortunately for me, the opposite mode of this wasn't her rule at all. She popped me twice in the face and told me to leave. I'll give it to her; she punched me well. I had two red marks on the side of my face that left her engagement ring imprints. I suppose the old saying of "If your woman doesn't hit you at least once that means she doesn't love you" is true. Her punches made me compare her to Oscar De La Hoya, but I was so mad at her that night that I packed a few things, got my bottle of vodka and walked out the door. I was worse than my own father. I left a 3 year-old and a 2 year-old alone with their mother.

My ma and her new husband were disappointed, but they let me stay with them. I didn't have a job, a wife or, kids. But I had a few things. My old car, free time and alcohol. Two years had passed. I found my way into that bar scene again...minus the guidance of Jesse. I admit, I had a score of beer-laden nights filled with dancing, drunken bar girls and people that I thought were my friends. Sherri and I still kept in touch. Down deep, we loved each other and we both knew we would be back together one day.

This part of the story is the final time that I saw a glowing light. It may be the weirdest story that you've ever heard. It may be unbelievable. It definitely is to me, but it is the weirdest, worst and saddest thing I've ever been through.

PART 14:

The last part of my story begins. It was around noon. My ma was a few minutes away, visiting her parents. Monte was at work. I was hungry, so I got dressed and decided to go get a pizza and a six-pack of beer. Nothing odd about that, huh? Well, that was going to change.

It took me about 30 minutes to get my food, beer and drive back to my "new house." I could smell the pizza beside me. I couldn't wait to take a bite of it and crack open a cold beer.

As I pulled up the drive way, I could see a brown delivery truck by the garage. I parked my car beside it, grabbed my lunch and noticed a blonde-headed woman wearing sunglasses knocking at the front door. She was an older woman. Well, when I say older, I mean about 40. She was attractive, so all of my "dirty man fantasies" began to rattle in my head. As I approached, she asked me if I was Monte Calvin. I told her that I wasn't, but he was my stepdad. The package was a vase full of lilies for my ma from Monte. That golden-haired delivery driver told me that all I had to do was sign for them and she'd be on her way. As I wrote my name on some sort of electronic pad, I began to notice everything about her. She was even better looking than I had thought. With her blonde hair and sunglasses twinkling in the light, no man could resist her.

Her name was Donna. It was woven by a yellow thread into her brown shirt. She stood about my heighth, 5' 10" or so, but she had a simple wedding ring on her left hand. I didn't care. This was a once in a lifetime opportunity. I had to take a chance.

As I finished writing my name, she said "Thank you" and began to walk back to her truck. This was my last shot.

I carelessly spoke. "Hey, Donna. Would you like a piece of my pizza and a cold beer. I just got them."

Donna responded. "How do you know my name?" I laughed and told her it was on her shirt. She giggled back and reticently said: "I can't drink while I'm at work, but that pizza smells nice and it is lunch time." I remember that mysterious hesitation in her voice from when I first asked Sherri on a date. My crazy risk may have worked. I told her that I can go inside and get her a can of soda. Donna accepted my foolish offer.

I handed her the pizza and asked if she wouldn't mind bringing it to the picnic table placed at the side of the house. She did just that as I brought the flowers inside and grabbed her an ice-cold can from the refrigerator. I walked outside toting a six-pack of beer in one hand and a can of soda in the other. I sat down beside her. My ma's house was maroon with white borders, but ALL of the houses on my ma's street were about 100 yards apart. Large trees lined the front and back yards. I wasn't afraid of being seen.

As we opened the pizza box, we both grabbed a slice but nothing was really said. It was what you would call "awkward." I ate a few slices, she ate two. Still, nothing was really said. I finished a little before her, popped open a beer and finally asked her:

"So, Donna. What's your story?"

She simply replied back: "Tell me your name first and then you can tell me YOUR story."

Due to my self-imposed loneliness and being on the verge of an incredible moment in "hook-up history", I just smiled and responded: "Well, I'm Payton James. I'm about to be 30. I went to college and moved back home. Kinda sad, huh?" I just told her the truth...kind of. I admit, I was just trying to cut my life story down so she would talk to me. But before I could say anything else, I saw a single tear run down the side of her face.

I asked her what was wrong. She spoke, "My doctor told me that I have breast cancer. They're going to have to remove my breasts. If that doesn't work, then it's chemotherapy for me. If that doesn't work, I may die. And by the way, my name is Donna Riley. I'm 44, live with my husband and kids. I have three of them: 16, 13 and 10. Thanks to this cancer, my jerk of a husband just may have the excuse to leave me. If I live, my husband will leave me. If I die, I will be leaving my 3 kids for good with that ass. What do I do, Payton?"

I didn't know what to say. I could tell her the truth, but who am I to say what will happen? I could lie and tell her that it would all be fine. I was flabbergasted. I couldn't say anything. I just wiped the tear from her face and softly gave her a hug. I needed to say something. Luckily, I didn't have to.

PART 15:

Right then, three black sedan cars with tinted windows drove by faster than I'd ever seen a vehicle drive down my ma's old road. Donna and I both looked at each other and wondered in confusion.

I simply said: "What the hell was that?"

She looked as baffled as I did. Then, a yellowish light came streaming at us from the clear sky above. It appeared to be far away at first, but kept getting closer and closer. It made no sound. We thought it may be a plane at first. Maybe an asteroid or some space debris, but the object made still produced no sound. Donna and I couldn't take our eyes off of it.

Through the glow around it, the object appeared to have a greyish, shiny surface. It had no smoke trail out of the back, no sound and falling at a tremendous speed. No one else seem to notice. [Not surprising since the house was surrounded by older people who never came out of their homes.] About 200 yards away in my neighbor's backyard, it slammed into the ground.

The earth shook and our ears were ringing. Donna and I were both terrified. We looked at the crash. Both of us knew we had to do something. I grabbed the keys to my old car out of my pants pocket. We both ran to my old car. She jumped into my passenger seat and we raced towards the site. I whipped my old car around and pulled out of my ma's driveway and into my neighbor's. We saw an old woman that owned the house peering out of her front door. I yelled at her to call 9-1-1 because I thought there had been a crash. I don't know if she ever called anyone. We never saw her again. I drove through the grass down that old lady's backyard towards the crash. Donna and I both jumped out of the car.

Part 16:

It was definitely a crashsite. The grass was burned, but it didn't look like a normal burn that you would expect to see. It was a whitish-purple color. It definitely was something like we had never seen. There was a strange shining metal like aluminum or tin foil on the ground surrounding a pile of torn up bodies. We thought the bodies were going to be disgusting. There laid a mass of bodies lying around, yet there was no blood. All of the arms and legs seemed to be severed with a clean saw. It was like a stack of mannequins scattered about. It was odd. Different than I thought any crash would be. The indention the object had left was about 30 yards across, about a yard deep and was in the shape of a perfect circle like I had thrown a bowling ball filled with little human limbs from a cliff. The smell was even weird; like a rotten banana with a pinch of asparagus. This was unreal.

Donna and I then noticed a movement in the center of the circle. There was an Asian boy with his mother. He could have been no more than 10, his mother about my age. We jumped down in the hole. Donna and I both ran through the debris and body limbs towards them. Once we removed the "metal" surrounding them, they both stood up. Neither one of them had a scratch on their bodies. I spoke to them, but they didn't understand a thing I said. They were speaking a language that I had never heard. At the same time, they both seemed as healthy as two robins making a nest. You could tell they were as confused as Donna and I were. All four of us just stood there staring blankly at each other. This didn't seem right, but a strange sensation came over my body. It was like I was taking acid without the trip. It was a feeling I had never felt before. I hate to say it, but it felt great.

Right then, the three black cars with tinted windows reappeared with a calvalry of large, dark green, military trucks behind them. I thought they had to be here to help. The vehicles raced to the circle where we stood. What appeared to be soldiers encased the crashsite with their guns in hand like we were criminals that had just robbed a bank. The soldiers told us not to move and put your arms in the air. This may be weirder than before. Why would they treat us like we all had done something wrong? Hell, Donna and I were just trying to help. Even though we really didn't, we didn't deserve this.

It wasn't five minutes and a tent was being put up around all around the entire site. Nine men in white bio suits with masks approached all four of us. My arms were still raised. I had always had stretch marks on my arms since I was once so fat, but they were gone. Instead of having that constant pain on my right side that I had felt for the last decade, a soothing sensation took over. I felt normal again. I asked Donna if she felt different.

Before she could respond, a man in one of those white suits told me: "Keep quiet, boy! Shut your mouth. There will be no talking."

Usually, I'd tell any man that said that to me to me to shut his mouth and go kiss a testicle, but I obeyed. For some reason, I kept quiet and did what he said. Maybe I was scared. I don't know. As they told us to remove all of our clothes, put them in a pile and cover of ourselves in these paper-thin blue "robes", the men asked us who had been in the crash.

In a trembling voice, I said, "The Asian kid and his mom had been in the crash, but this woman and I weren't."

In time, he undoubtedly asked what the woman and I were doing there. Donna and I didn't really know. She said that she was just delivering a package to my house and eating lunch. We finally just told him we were trying to help.

The man spoke: "You should've just minded your business."

Not much was said after that. We were standing there half naked under a tent in my neighbor's yard. I told him the facts as other people in bio suits scanned our bodies with some sort of handheld gadget with a blinking red light. All I wanted was a piece of pizza and a cold beer. I guess drinking can kill you, huh?

The men told us all to enter into some kind of car that looked like a white RV. We all entered in our blue. paper robes and sat on little metal benches. All of these different thoughts entered into my head. All I could think about was Sherri standing there all alone with my two kids. I would give anything to go back to her. She was the mother of my kids and my beautiful wife. She was perfect and I was the idiot that left her alone. If I could ever get back to my life, I'd give anything to make her happy again.

FINAL:

Unfortunately, that never happened. We were driven to some sort of unknown area hours away. I never knew what happened to my saint of a mother. I hope she's living a great life with Monte. I don't know what happened to Sherri and my kids. I hope they found a new life with a "good man" and are happy. I never saw Donna or any of my friends again. I was taken away from my life. I was forced into a room with a glowing light from the ceiling. Everyday, I think of my family. I can see their faces in that glowing white light above me. My ma's undying love, Sherri's beauty and my kids' eyes.

That was the last time I would ever see a glowing light.

THE END

Travis Waters is a simple voice of the people. Waters is a 40 year-old man with a plain university degree in psychology that has experienced many of the quandaries in this book. As one may read this, you may relate to many of the passions that fuel the normal person.

Printed in the United States
By Bookmasters